Cover layout by V. Burke

Editing by Renee Waring
Guardian Proofreading Services

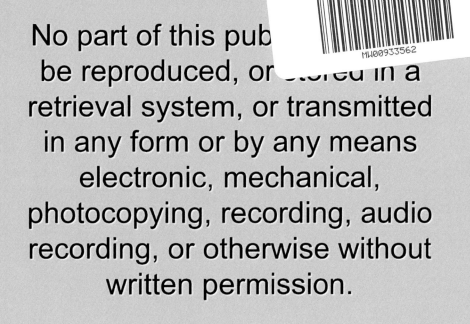

Dedicated to the loving and caring staff at Animal Adventure Park whose unwavering devotion to the animals in their care, warmed our hearts.

Proceeds from this publication will support Animal Adventure Park and Giraffe Conservation Foundation

April didn't know how special her baby was. She spent her days doing what giraffes do...

and making hay showers,

and playing with her partner, Oliver,

and waiting for her baby to arrive.

One day, the park where April lived put a camera in her pen and the whole world met April!

the world took notice!

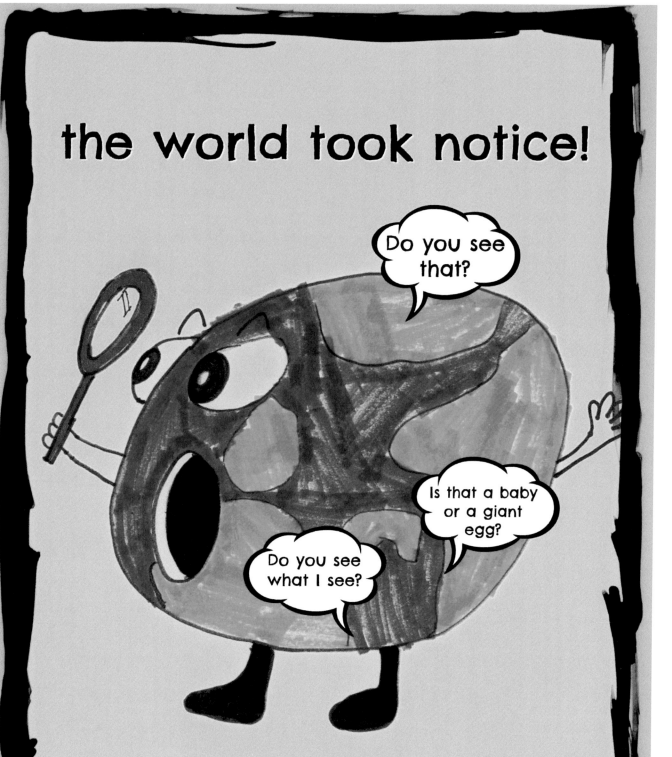

Some people joked that April was going to lay an egg, and some days her tummy looked like a giant egg, but April knew her baby was growing like babies should.

and the world
watched and smiled.

At naptime, April would put her head on her tummy and hum to her baby...

and the world
hummed along.

Her baby grew bigger, and wiggled and squiggled, doing cartwheels inside April's tummy...

and the whole world waited...

Until one day, a tiny hoof appeared...

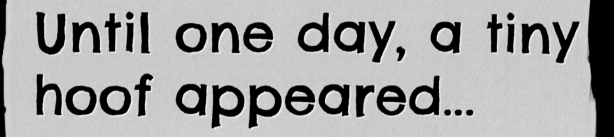

and the world held its breath for April's baby.

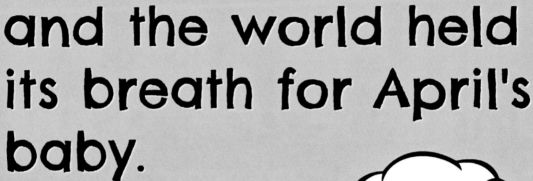

I'm turning blue in the planet.

On a special spring day, April and Oliver greeted their baby,

But this isn't the end of April's story, it's just the beginning. See, April and her baby are doing something amazing.

They are teaching the world how important it is to take care of the giraffes in Africa and how help is needed to ensure their survival for future generations...

and the world
is listening.

April doesn't know she and her baby are special. She, and baby, and Oliver just do what giraffes do...

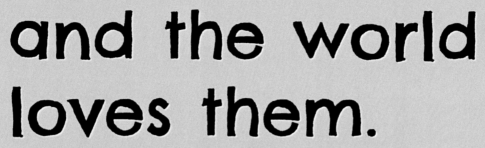

and the world loves them.

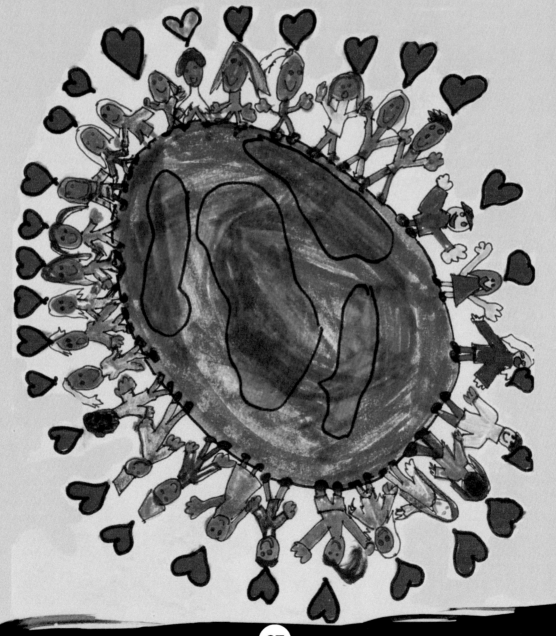

The End

We'd like to thank
Animal Adventure Park
and
Giraffe Conservation
Foundation
for their truly inspiring work.

www.animaladventurepark.com

www.giraffeconservation.org

45024183R00021

Made in the USA
Middletown, DE
22 June 2017